MY DUCKY BUDDY
Mi Amigo El Pato

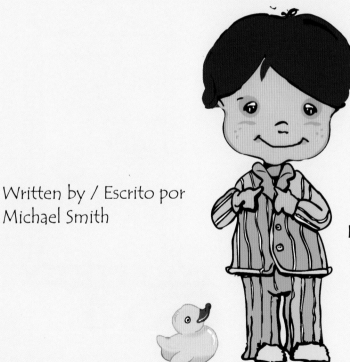

Written by / Escrito por
Michael Smith

Illustrated by / Ilustrado por
Octavio Oliva

East West Discovery Press
Manhattan Beach, California

My rubber ducky takes a swim.
He's my buddy in the bath.
I'm playing with him.

Mi patito de hule quiere nadar.

Es mi amigo en el baño.

Con él quiero jugar.

He rides the bubbles,
then takes a dip.

Se monta en las burbujas,
y se zambulle.

He floats on the water,
then takes a sip.

Flota en el agua
y un traguito engulle.

My rubber ducky is hungry for lunch,
and finds a nice fish to munch.

Mi patito de hule quiere comer y encuentra un pececito para morder.

He is my buddy in the bubbles,
a friend with no troubles.

En las burbujas es mi amigo,
él es muy feliz conmigo.

Bobbing up and down,
he never sinks.

He tastes the water,
but never really drinks.

Flota y flota
y no se hunde.

No traga el agua;
la guarda en el buche.

He is soft and squishy
and made of rubber.

When I push in his tummy,
it pops back like blubber.

Está hecho de hule
y es suave y blandito.

Si aprieto su barriga,
hace un ruidito.

When I dry off and get ready for bed,
I think about him.
He is stuck in my head.

Cuando me seco y me voy a la cama,
pienso en él cuando me pongo
la piyama.

Up come the covers.
It's time to sleep.

But ducky is there
while I try to count sheep.

Me cubren con mantas.
Es hora de dormir.

Cuando cuento ovejitas,
mi patito está allí.

What a wonderful sight.
What do I see?

¡Qué maravilloso!
¿Qué es esto aquí?

Oh, my rubber ducky,
                    you're back with me.

Oh, patito de hule,
                    otra vez junto a mí.

23

For my niece and nephew, Jasmine and Justin, and their ducky buddy.
—Michael Smith

To my loving wife, Vianney, and our son, Oliver.
—Octavio Oliva

Published by East West Discovery Press
P.O. Box 3585, Manhattan Beach, CA 90266
Phone: 310-545-3730, Fax: 310-545-3731
E-mail: info@eastwestdiscovery.com
Website: www.eastwestdiscovery.com

Written by Michael Smith
Illustrated by Octavio Oliva
Edited by Marcie Rouman
Spanish translation by Redactores en Red
Design and production by Icy Smith and Jennifer Thomas

ISBN-13: 978-0-9821675-5-7 Hardcover
Library of Congress Control Number: 2010938864
First Bilingual English and Spanish Edition 2011
Printed in China
Published in the United States of America